MUSICAL

STORIES FROM EAST HIGH #12

BONJOUR, WILDCATS!

By N.B. Grace

Based on the Disney Channel Original Movie
"High School Musical," Written by Peter Barsocchini
Based on "High School Musical 2," Written by Peter Barsocchini
Based on Characters Created by Peter Barsocchini

DISNEY PRESS
New York

CHAPTER ONE

"**G**ood morning! Welcome to another *wonderful* Monday!" Ms. Darbus called out over the hubbub of her homeroom class.

Ms. Darbus clapped her hands for silence. "Settle down, everyone." There were a few groans, and then the noise finally subsided. "Thank you," Ms. Darbus said. She added drily, "I know Mondays are terribly exciting, but we must control our extreme glee at being back at school after what was undoubtedly a long, boring, practically endless weekend."

"Yeah, Saturdays just seem to go on *forever*," Chad Danforth joked. "I mean, there's never anything to do! Well, except catch a movie."

"Or shoot some hoops," his friend, Troy Bolton, chimed in.

"Or play video games," Jason Cross added.

"Or maybe go for a bike ride," Zeke Baylor finished.

But Chad shook his head, pretending to look pained at all these suggestions. "No, guys, face it, weekends are endless deserts of time, just waiting to be filled with pointless activity." He folded his hands on his desk and looked earnestly at their homeroom teacher. "You're so right, Ms. Darbus. I can hardly wait to get to calculus class."

Across the aisle, Taylor McKessie rolled her eyes. Chad grinned at her and said, "I know, I know. You actually *are* looking forward to calculus."

"We're going to learn about the Riemann

integral today, so, yes, Chad, I am looking forward to it," Taylor replied.

Gabriella Montez glanced over at Troy and caught his eye. They both grinned. It was always fun to see Chad tease Taylor and then watch Taylor pretend she didn't like it.

"Well, it *is* fun to come to school when you can see all your friends," Gabriella said under her breath so that only Troy would hear it. "Especially since this is sometimes the only place where that happens!"

He gave her an understanding wink. Troy and Gabriella usually hung out quite a bit in their free time, but the last two weekends had been so packed with basketball games, family gatherings, and homework that they had only managed a couple of hurried phone conversations. "At least nothing's going on this weekend," he whispered back, just as the late bell rang.

Ms. Darbus rapped on her desk. "Actually, this Monday is a little more exciting than most," she said to the class, "because we have a surprise in store—"

Before she could finish, Sharpay Evans and her brother, Ryan, bounded breathlessly into the room. Sharpay was wearing a pink skirt covered with blue flowers, a short white jacket over a turquoise T-shirt, and a long purple scarf. Ryan's outfit was more subdued in comparison, but he had decided that a brown tweed fedora was a good match for tan pants and a pink-and-white striped shirt. They both looked good, and they knew it.

Sharpay and Ryan paused by Ms. Darbus's desk, clearly enjoying the feeling that all eyes were on them. They even seemed to be striking a pose, as if they had just made their entrance onto a Broadway stage.

"You're late," Ms. Darbus said, frowning. Even though Sharpay and Ryan were the stars of the Drama Club, and even though Ms. Darbus was the drama teacher, she still didn't like tardiness. "And I must say, I'm very surprised at you both! Surely your years of theater training under my tutelage, no less, would have taught you that punctuality is a key component to success!"

"Yes, you're right and we're soooo sorry!" Sharpay said, her eyes widening in dismay. "But we have an incredibly good reason!"

Ryan nodded eagerly. "We just happened to be walking past Principal Matsui's office," he broke in. "And Mr. Matsui just happened to see us. And then he just happened to say—"

"That I was the perfect person to introduce a new student to our homeroom!" Sharpay interrupted, shooting an irritated glance at her brother.

Ryan bit his lip and took a couple of steps back. He knew better than to try to steal Sharpay's spotlight, but sometimes he just couldn't help himself. Like now, when they had such an exciting announcement to make!

"And that new student is"—Sharpay flung open the classroom door with all the dramatic flair she could muster—"Jean-Luc Laurent, from Paris, France!"

Everyone in the class leaned forward in their seats as Jean-Luc walked in with an easy stride.

"*Bonjour,*" he said. "I mean, hello."

Gabriella couldn't help exchanging a quick glance with Taylor, who gave her a look that said that she, too, was impressed. Jean-Luc had dark brown hair, brown eyes, and a confident smile. He didn't seem at all nervous as he stood in front of a room full of strangers.

Gabriella looked around and noticed that every girl in the class was leaning forward a little and looking interested.

"*Bonjour!* We are, er, *très content* to have you here!" Ms. Darbus cried as she rushed forward to shake his hand. Over her shoulder, she added, "*Très content* means very happy, class."

"I would be *très content* not to have to learn another language in homeroom," Chad muttered. "Since I'm already completely *ocupado* with Spanish class!"

Jason snickered, but fortunately Ms. Darbus did not hear Chad's comment.

"It is a wonderful, wonderful opportunity for us to have a foreign exchange student here, especially one from France!" Ms. Darbus said. "For centuries, the world has looked to France for its culture, its art, its music, its *joie de vivre*! That means joy of living, class, and I'm sure we will all be thrilled to learn even more about Jean-Luc's country during his time here."

"*Merci,*" Jean-Luc said politely. "That is, thank you. But I am interested in learning all about *your* country. I have dreamed of visiting the United States of America since I was a very little boy. And now, here I am!"

Ms. Darbus glanced at her watch. "We have a few minutes before the morning announcements," she said. "Why don't you tell us a little bit about yourself?"

It was the kind of question that would have flustered most people, Gabriella thought as she gave Jean-Luc a sympathetic glance.

But East High's newest student merely

nodded and said calmly, "Well, as Sharpay said, I'm from Paris—"

"But he was born in Lyons," Sharpay interrupted eagerly. "He has two younger sisters and a baby brother, his father is a lawyer, his mother works for the French government and is traveling around the United States on a fact-finding tour, which is why he's here at East High for the next two weeks. He wanted to get a taste of life at an American high school. He'll be sitting in on classes in algebra, U.S. history, English, and biology. Oh, and he speaks three languages. French, of course, English, and German, plus he's studying Italian—"

Chad raised his hand just as Sharpay paused to take a breath. "Excuse me, but are you going to let him say anything for himself in any of those three languages he speaks?" he asked politely.

Sharpay glared at him as the class erupted into laughter. "And *I* am going to be Jean-Luc's guide for the day," she finished proudly. "Principal Matsui asked me to introduce him to everyone and make him feel welcome." She turned to smile warmly at Jean-Luc. "I learned so much about him just on the short walk from the principal's office, and I'm sure I'll find out so much more as I show him around the school."

"Well, perhaps you should start by showing him to a seat," Ms. Darbus said. "I think there's an empty desk here in the front row, next to Kelsi."

As Jean-Luc nodded and sat down, Gabriella glanced at her friend, Kelsi Nielsen, and saw her staring intently down at her desk. Gabriella lifted one eyebrow in surprise. She and Kelsi were in the same French class, and she knew how much Kelsi loved to talk about French music and art. She would have thought that Kelsi would be thrilled to meet Jean-Luc, but she looked as if she barely knew he was there.

A squawk from the PA system interrupted Gabriella's thoughts. Principal Matsui's voice boomed through the room with the morning announcements.

Gabriella sighed and settled back in her seat to listen. Although she seemed to be the only person who was paying attention, she thought, as she glanced around the room. Chad was drawing a comic superhero in his notebook, Jason had his head on his desk, Zeke was yawning, and even Troy was staring at the ceiling and humming quietly.

She snuck another peek at Jean-Luc.

He was listening closely to the announcements, clearly much more interested than anyone else.

Well, of course, she thought. Even hearing the week's lunch menu—Mr. Matsui had reached Thursday, which would, once again, involve some mysterious form of meat loaf—would seem interesting if you were in a different country. And if you hadn't listened to the exact same lunch menu every single Monday for the last year.

Gabriella tapped her pencil on her desk as her eyes continued to roam around the room.

Kelsi, she noticed, continued to focus her gaze firmly on the floor, and she was sitting very still. In fact, she barely seemed to be breathing. Gabriella frowned slightly. She'd have to catch her friend after class and ask if something was wrong. True, Kelsi was rather shy, but she seemed off in her own world today.

". . . And finally, I'd like to remind everyone about this semester's talent show, which will be held next Friday," the principal said. "I know many of you are participating in this stellar event, and I want to wish you the best of luck. And I'd like to encourage everyone to attend to support your fellow Wildcats. Remember, your applause will determine which contestants make it to the final round—and who will win first prize!"

"Go, Kelsi!" Chad yelled. "You've already got my vote."

Ms. Darbus held up one hand. "Please wait until—"

". . . And that's the end of the morning

announcements," Mr. Matsui concluded. "Have a great week, East High! Go Wildcats!"

Ms. Darbus dropped her hand. "Although I don't want to encourage emotional outbursts—" She gave Chad a hard stare, and he ducked his head, abashed. "I must agree with Mr. Danforth. I certainly wish Kelsi the best with her piano piece, as well as Sharpay Evans, who will be singing a brilliant solo. You are all quite talented, and I'm sure that we'll be treated to a wonderful evening of entertainment, no matter who wins."

Sharpay tossed her blond hair back and said loudly, "Of course we're all talented. But someone has to win!"

Across the aisle, Ryan rolled his eyes ever so slightly. He knew exactly who Sharpay was referring to with that "we"—she meant herself. That was the way she had always been. In the past, Ryan had shared the stage with her in every musical, every play, every talent show, every competition. True, she'd left him out of her all-girls' group in East High's Battle of the Bands.

But other than that little hiccup, they had always performed as a team.

So when the date for the talent show had been announced, they'd sat down to discuss what they would sing. But for the first time ever, Ryan pointed out something he should have noticed long ago. "You know, Sharpay," he had said, "you always get top billing in the program."

She had looked at him blankly. "Of course," she had said, as if he'd just stated something terribly obvious, like "the sky is often blue."

"Well . . ." He hesitated, then forged on, "Why is that, exactly?"

"*I* am the star!" she replied. "Of course, you are quite talented, too—"

"Gee, thanks," Ryan grumbled. "That's nice of you."

"But let's face it," she went on, as if she hadn't heard him. "*I'm* the one people come to see."

For some reason, after years of playing second banana to Sharpay, it was that simple statement that made Ryan snap. "Fine!" he'd said. "You can sing all by yourself this time! Good luck!" And he had stormed out of the room.

Now, as Sharpay smiled smugly in the sure knowledge that she would win, Ryan had to admit that he regretted giving up a chance at yet another prize.

But then Sharpay's words—*I'm the one people come to see!*—seemed to echo in his ears. Ryan turned his head away from Sharpay and stared out the window. What's the use of getting another trophy for my room? he thought. Especially since it would only be for singing backup . . . again.

Across the room, Gabriella was also ignoring Sharpay. She knew all too well how Sharpay would take every chance to grab center stage, even if it was only here, in Ms. Darbus's home-room. So Gabriella tuned her out and turned her attention back to Kelsi, who was still staring at the floor. And, she noticed, Kelsi was blushing.

Suddenly, Gabriella understood. Kelsi was nervous about the competition! Gabriella smiled to herself and shook her head slightly. She had never known anyone who was so talented and yet so modest! She would have to say something encouraging to Kelsi to let her know that she shouldn't be afraid. She was sure to come out on top, no matter how good the other contestants were.

The bell rang, and the students jumped up. Gabriella gathered her books and headed for the door.

She looked over her shoulder and saw Troy right behind her.

"Hey, stranger," she said, smiling.

He smiled back. "Hey, yourself. How was your mom's birthday party?"

She rolled her eyes. "Fattening. How was your cousin's ballet recital?"

He chuckled. "Long. What are you doing tonight? Maybe we could get together and go over those trig questions?"

Gabriella felt a warm glow inside that had nothing to do with her sincere appreciation of trigonometry. "Sounds good."

She glanced past him, somewhat surprised that they hadn't already been engulfed by a horde of students escaping from homeroom into the halls. Her eyes widened. At least a dozen girls were clustered around Jean-Luc's desk, eagerly asking him questions.

Chad slouched toward Troy and Gabriella, looking disgruntled. "What does everybody see in that dude, anyway?"

Gabriella bit her lip. There was an obvious answer, but she didn't think it was one that Chad wanted to hear. "Well . . ."

"Oh, come on, it *is* pretty cool to meet someone from another country," Troy pointed out. "And anyway, not everybody is talking to him." He smiled at Kelsi, who was edging her way past them. "Hey, Kelsi, are you excited about the talent show?"

"What?" For a second, she looked as if she had no idea what he was talking about. Then her face cleared and she said hurriedly, "Oh, the contest! Yes, I'm ready. I mean, I'm a little

16

nervous, but a tiny bit of stage fright is actually a good thing. . . ."

"You'll do great," Troy said warmly.

Kelsi blushed. "Thanks."

As she headed off down the hall, Gabriella said to Troy, "I saw Kelsi looking a little distant in class. I thought she might be worried about the competition. It was nice of you to encourage her like that."

"Hey, I was only speaking the truth," Troy said, but he looked pleased at the compliment. "Come on, I'll walk you to class and you can fill me in on all the desserts you and your mom had at her party."

CHAPTER TWO

"All right, guys, keep hustling out there!" Coach Bolton was pacing the sidelines and staring intently at his basketball players that afternoon. The Wildcats were practicing for their next big game against West High. "You're looking good, let's keep it going!"

Troy nodded to show his dad he had heard him, then stole the ball from Zeke and sprinted down the court. Even as he stopped, pivoted, and passed the ball to Jason, he noticed that Sharpay,

Ryan, and Jean-Luc had just entered the gym and were headed for the bleachers. Hmm, he thought, that's odd. Sharpay and Ryan usually spend all their after-school time in the theater.

Just then, Jason lofted the ball toward the basket and missed, snapping Troy's attention back to the court. Troy dashed forward to recover the ball, but Chad got there first.

"You're going to have to be faster than that, cap!" Chad said with a grin.

Coach Bolton blew his whistle for a break. As the Wildcats headed for the water fountain, Chad nodded toward the bleachers, where a half-dozen girls were hovering around Jean-Luc.

"Dude, check that out," Chad said to Troy, frowning slightly. "The guy's only been here for half a day, and he's already got an entourage." He took a sip of water, then moved aside for Troy to take his turn and went back to staring at Jean-Luc. "The girls in this school act like they've never seen someone from another country before!"

Zeke was standing to one side staring darkly at Sharpay, his arms crossed firmly over his chest. "She's just interested in him because he sounds French," he muttered. "Big deal. If I had been born in Paris, I would sound French, too!"

Troy shrugged, laughing. "Hey, maybe you guys should start working on an accent," he suggested. "Add some intrigue to your profile, you know what I mean? Girls like a little mystery."

Jason jogged over to them in time to overhear this. "Really? They do?" he asked.

"Sure," Chad said. "In fact, I'm going to start reading up on my Sherlock Holmes."

They were still laughing when Coach Bolton blew his whistle, letting them know that break was over and that they had to head back to center court.

In the bleachers, Sharpay inched a little closer to Jean-Luc. "Isn't this fun?" She turned and gave him a big smile. "I just love sports, don't you?"

She hurriedly crossed her fingers behind her

back as she uttered that little white lie. Actually, she hadn't even known the differences among football, basketball, and baseball until last year. Then she became a lot more interested—in basketball, at least—when she realized that Troy Bolton was the captain of the team.

"Especially basketball," she went on. "I've been a basketball fan for ages!"

Sharpay heard a little snort of amusement on her left. She turned to give Ryan an icy look, and he quickly wiped the smile from his face.

"Me, too," Jean-Luc said, oblivious to the little drama that had just played out. "So, you must go to all the games?"

Sharpay hesitated. "Well, I would if I *could*," she said. "But since I'm usually the star of every play, musical, and talent show at East High, my schedule is far too busy. Rehearsals, costume fittings, hair and makeup tests . . ." She sighed. "You know how it is—one's art must always come first."

"Oh, yes, of course." Jean-Luc nodded. "That

is unfortunate for you, though, isn't it? It looks like the Wildcats are a very good team." At that moment, Chad managed to steal the ball from Troy. As he made a break for the basket, there was a cheer from the stands, and Jean-Luc turned away from Sharpay to watch the action, an eager expression on his face.

Sharpay pursed her lips. It was one thing to be interested in sports but another thing to ignore her completely in favor of watching sweaty basketball players running around and bouncing a stupid ball! She crossed her arms and looked around the gym.

The seats behind them were surprisingly full. Sharpay had no idea that this many people were interested in watching the Wildcats practice. She glanced at the audience just long enough to note that most of them were girls who seemed to be looking in her direction. She tossed her hair, pleased at the attention. Then her gaze moved to the East High cheerleaders, who were on the side of the court working on their routines.

Sharpay watched them critically for a few moments. She was always interested in any kind of performance. Their smiles gleamed as they shouted out chants and cartwheeled across the floor. Their energy level was high. Their movements were precisely coordinated. Sharpay gave a little nod of approval.

Then Wiley the Wildcat, East High's mascot, bounced into the gym and started jumping around on the sidelines and waving his arms. A small group of students cheered and clapped as the mascot did a handspring that ended in a dramatic split.

"Way to go, Wiley!" a boy sitting in the top bleacher yelled. "Let's see you do a dive-and-slide!"

The mascot waved in acknowledgment, then moved to the far end of the bleachers. He held his hand above his eyes, gauging the distance, then wiggled his body, preparing to try an extremely difficult move. Some students started chanting, "Go, go, go!" He started running. As he reached the middle of the gym, he took a flying dive forward and slid on his belly for at least ten feet.

The gym erupted in cheers as Wiley stood up and took a bow. Several bows, in fact.

Sharpay rolled her eyes at the ridiculous, furry mascot. True, sports mascots were not usually asked to give performances with depth and feeling. But why did they have to be so cartoonish? And why did audiences love them so much?

"That person in the furry costume is quite funny, isn't he?" Jean-Luc said. "He's like a mime, but he can't even use his face to communicate! That must be very difficult."

"I suppose," Sharpay replied. "If you like that sort of thing."

"I do," Jean-Luc said, clearly missing the disdain in her voice. "But, please, can you tell me . . . what is the name of the creature?"

From the other side of Sharpay, Ryan leaned forward to answer. "That's Wiley!" he said eagerly.

Jean-Luc looked puzzled.

Sharpay heaved a deep sigh, then began explaining. "He's our mascot. You know, because we're the Wildcats. He runs around and does silly things and tries to get the crowd excited."

"I see." Jean-Luc was nodding. "How does a person get this job?"

"You have to try out," Ryan said. "It's very competitive. Lots of students want to be Wiley the Wildcat."

Sharpay shook her head. "I can't understand it myself! After all, people come to watch the game and *maybe* the cheerleaders! Wiley's a supporting role at best. I mean, why do all that work if you're not the star?"

Jean-Luc turned his attention back to the mascot, who was standing behind the cheerleaders and mimicking their dance moves. The crowd had been clapping and yelling along with the cheerleaders, but once Wiley started doing his own exaggerated version of the cheers, everyone started laughing again.

"Even so, he is rather funny," Jean-Luc said with a shrug. He laughed as Wiley grabbed a cheerleader's pom-poms and jumped into the air. "And he seems to be getting most of the attention, too."

"Really?" Ryan turned to watch the mascot's antics more closely. "You're right!" he said after a moment. "When he's on the floor, no one can take their eyes off him!" He watched Wiley for a moment longer. "*He's* the star!" Ryan whispered to himself, so softly that no one else heard him.

Sharpay turned to smile brightly at Jean-Luc. "Enough talk about large, furry cartoon characters! Tell me, Jean-Luc, what are you most looking forward to doing during your stay in our country? Perhaps you'd like to attend the symphony with us next week? We have season tickets, and I'm sure my father would let you use his." She turned the wattage of her smile up a few degrees. "The program is going to include Debussy, Berlioz—"

"Ah, French composers," Jean-Luc said in a bored voice.

"*Oui!*" she cried. "You would feel right at home!"

"But I am so interested in *your* country," he said. "In fact, I was wondering if maybe I could learn more about basketball!"

Sharpay's eyes narrowed as she watched the players bounding around the hardwood floor, giving each other high fives after successful plays, and joking during time-outs. She bit her lip, thinking hard. And then her face brightened as she got a brilliant idea.

"How lucky that you mentioned your interest in basketball to me, of all people!" she said.

"Oh?" Jean-Luc turned his head to give her his full attention. "Why is that?"

"It just so happens that I'm very close friends with Troy Bolton, the captain of the team," she answered brightly. "I'm sure that if *I* ask him, he would agree to teach you."

"Well, that would be wonderful," Jean-Luc

said, grinning. "I would love to go home and show all my friends the moves I learned here in America! They would be very impressed."

"Then it's a deal," Sharpay said. "I'll talk to Troy after practice. I'm sure he'll do it for *moi*."

"Everybody's looking good, let's keep it up!" Coach Bolton clapped his hands as he paced up and down the sidelines. The practice was going well, but he knew how tough West High was. He couldn't afford to let his team take anything for granted. "Fight for that rebound, Chad! Troy, keep the guys moving! Jason, Zeke, let's see some hustle out there!"

He was watching every move his players made with intense concentration. He was watching so carefully, in fact, that he didn't even notice Wiley the Wildcat on the sidelines.

Inside the mascot's costume was Andrew Everline, a sophomore who had nabbed the job in the fall after a tough competition. Ever since, Andrew had been working hard to take his performance as a mascot to the highest level possible. He spent evenings studying game tapes in the basement. He ignored the football and basketball teams who were playing and focused all of his attention on the few precious glimpses of the mascots in the background.

He knew the moves of all the great mascots: the San Diego Chicken, the Philly Phanatic, the Pirate Parrot. But he had higher ambitions than merely copying someone else's moves. Andrew wanted to develop his own style—one that would set him apart from every other mascot in the game.

That meant hard work, and lots of it. He had to be able to execute every move with precision and flair.

This afternoon, for example, he was trying to perfect a series of backflips. He had learned how to do one backflip at a time, but he was determined to work his way up to three in a row. That would get the crowd cheering! That would be something to be proud of!

Just as he was thinking that, he launched into a flip—and slammed into something hard, landing on the gym floor with a thud.

"Ugh," Andrew grunted as he felt the breath knocked out of him. His ankle twisted painfully underneath him.

For one seemingly endless moment, he felt a surge of panic. Then his lungs filled with air, and he heard the worst thing a mascot could ever hear: a silent crowd. In that instant, he knew what he had to do: he had to reassure them all that everything was okay. Because no matter the pain, no matter the shock, no matter what happened to him, he was their mascot!

Quickly, he began flailing his arms in what he hoped was a comical manner. He turned his head to look at the bleachers through the costume's narrow eyeholes. He spotted expressions of worry on many faces, but as he wiggled around trying to stand, he saw them gradually disappear. Good! he thought.

He managed to push himself up to a sitting

position. He put both hands to his head, then threw them in the air miming dismay. A few people grinned. Just what he'd been hoping for.

Then he stood up and hopped around on one foot, pretending to be in great pain. Well, he wasn't pretending that much. But then he heard people laughing, and that sweet sound eased the throbbing in his right ankle.

Inside the stuffy Wildcat head, Andrew grinned. This was what separated the good mascots from the great ones, he thought. This was what legends were made of. . . .

Then he accidentally put his right foot on the ground. A stab of pain shot through his leg. Even though he was in agony, Andrew managed to wave his arms around like a cartoon character whose big toe was just hit by a mallet, hoping he could make it to the exit before he fainted.

Halfway to the door, he saw Coach Bolton gingerly pick himself up from where he'd been sprawled on the floor.

"Nice backflip, Andrew," the coach said,

holding a hand to his back and wincing. "Maybe it would help if you looked where you were going next time, though."

Andrew held out his arms in an elaborate shrug of apology, then gave the coach a big hug.

A wave of laughter spread through the bleachers.

Coach Bolton grinned and eased his way out of the hug. "All right, Andrew, I've got to get back to practice," he said. "You have a good day now."

Andrew snapped off a quick salute, then began hobbling toward the door. His practice was over for today, but he couldn't remember a time when he had felt happier.

Coach Bolton, shaking his head, watched as Wiley the Wildcat left the gym. Back in the days when he was dreaming of his future and hoping that it would include playing or coaching the game he loved, he never would have imagined that he'd risk injury by colliding with the school mascot. Fortunately, he hadn't gotten anything worse than a banged-up elbow. He rubbed it absently as he turned back to the practice.

"All right, guys, let's finish up with ten sprints, then you're good to go," he yelled.

Troy led the players to the end of the court. "Okay, on the count of three," he called out. "One, two, three!"

The thud of sneakers hitting the floor echoed off the gym walls. Coach Bolton watched with satisfaction. His team was in great condition and filled with school spirit. He had a very good feeling about their next game—not that he would ever say that out loud. Coach Bolton never did anything that might jinx his team.

Suddenly, he became aware that someone was standing to his right, waiting to talk to him. He turned and saw Sharpay beside him with a student he didn't recognize.

"Hi, coach!" Sharpay said. "Have you met Jean-Luc Laurent? He's an exchange student from France. He'll be here at East High for a few weeks, and I'm his guide."

"Hi, there." Coach Bolton held out his hand. "Principal Matsui mentioned that you were going to be here at East High for a little while. I hope you're enjoying yourself so far."

Jean-Luc shook the coach's hand. "Very much, thank you. I especially like watching the team—"

"Jean-Luc is a huge basketball fan!" Sharpay interrupted. "In fact, that's why I brought him over to meet you. I—I mean, *he*—would like to ask you a huge favor!"

"What's that?" Coach Bolton asked. He wanted to sound friendly, but he was wary. From what he had seen, Sharpay knew how to turn on the charm to get what she wanted. Now she was positively twinkling at him. It must be a pretty big favor, he thought, bracing himself.

"Well, Jean-Luc would really, really like to learn how to play basketball," Sharpay went on earnestly. "And I know that Troy is the best player on the team. So I—I mean, *Jean-Luc*—

was wondering if maybe Troy could coach him a little bit in his free time."

Coach Bolton hesitated. "I'd have to ask Troy. He's pretty busy right now with the big game coming up, and his schoolwork and everything—"

"Oh, but I am so interested in the basketball!" Jean-Luc said eagerly. "I understand that I couldn't play in a game, but even practicing and learning from the players would help me really experience the American culture."

"Yeah, I see what you mean," Coach Bolton said. "Hey, listen, I think it's great that you want to learn more about the game! Let me see what I can do."

Troy trotted off the court, still breathing hard from the series of sprints. He couldn't wait to get to the locker room, change, and head home. If he finished all of his homework before dinner, he thought he could watch a DVD before it was time to go to bed.

"Troy, do you have a minute?" Coach Bolton gestured him over to the sidelines.

"Sure, Dad." Troy stopped. "What's up?"

Quickly, Coach Bolton told him about Jean-Luc's request. "So, I'd like to know your thoughts, as the team captain."

"He's never played before, right?"

Coach Bolton nodded.

Troy thought for a moment. He had been looking forward to having a little more free time after the hectic schedule of the last two weeks. He wanted to chill with his buddies, practice his guitar, and, of course, hang out with Gabriella. On the other hand, playing basketball was always fun.

"Well, I've never tried to teach a beginner," he said. "But it's cool that he wants to learn to play. And Ms. Darbus was saying that we should help Jean-Luc feel at home. . . ."

"Exactly." Mr. Bolton gave Troy an approving nod. "As long as you think you can keep up with all your other responsibilities."

"I think I can fit it in," he said. "Maybe we could issue him a uniform and have him take part in practices, too, just to get a feel for it. He could even sit on the bench during a game."

"Great idea." Troy's dad clapped him on the shoulder. "Thanks, Troy. I know this is more work for you, but I'm glad to see you're willing to go the extra mile."

"Sure, Dad, no problem," Troy said. As his father walked away, Chad crawled out from under the bleachers, where he had recovered one of the extra basketballs, and bounded over to Troy.

"So, you've been roped into spending time with the foreign exchange student," he said, grinning. "Man, with your calendar so full, you're never going to see Gabriella!"

"He's only going to be here for two weeks," Troy said. "Hey, maybe you could help me coach him."

"Thanks, but no thanks," Chad said. "I'm not ready to join the Jean-Luc fan club. It's already got enough members."

"What does that mean?" Troy stopped to look directly into his friend's eyes. "Why are you so down on the guy?"

Chad shrugged. "I'm not. I just don't see why he's getting all this attention. I mean, did you see all those girls at practice? I bet half of them didn't even know East High had a basketball team until today! And let me tell you something else—they weren't here to watch us. They were here to fall all over Jean-Luc!"

Troy grinned. "Watch out, Chad, you're beginning to sound like Sharpay," he said teasingly. "Always wanting the spotlight."

Chad stopped and looked into Troy's eyes, his expression horrified. "You're right! This is terrible! My body must have been taken over by an evil diva of some kind!" He clutched Troy's shoulder and whispered weakly, "Help . . . me . . . *please.*"

Laughing, Troy shook his head. "I would, but I've got to get Jean-Luc a uniform. Listen, Chad, seriously, would you mind helping me coach

Jean-Luc? I could use another player to help show him the ropes."

"Ah, man . . ." Chad grimaced at the thought.

"The only way to dispel the curse of self-centeredness is to help another in need," Troy said, trying to sound like a mystical guru. From the way Chad rolled his eyes, Troy could tell his impression was far from hitting the mark.

But it did its job in the only way he cared about, because Chad shrugged and said, "Okay, okay. But only because I don't want to end up like Sharpay!"

CHAPTER THREE

The next day during study hall, Gabriella and Taylor headed to the library. Each one was loaded down with an armful of books.

"How are you doing on that history paper?" Taylor asked. "I haven't even started writing yet!"

Gabriella sighed. "I've gotten as far as an outline, but that's it," she admitted. "My problem is I can't stop researching! It seems like there's always one more book to read, you know?"

"Tell me about it," Taylor said ruefully. As they entered the library, she spotted Kelsi sitting at a paper-strewn table by herself, reading a book. "Hi, Kelsi. Can we join you?"

Kelsi looked up, startled. "Sure," she said. She quickly put the book facedown on the table and began shifting nervously through her papers. "I was just, um, taking some notes for that history paper."

Gabriella and Taylor exchanged glances.

"That's what we're working on, too," Gabriella said, sitting down. "What topic did you choose?"

"How the French and American revolutions were similar and how they were different," Kelsi said.

"Wow," Taylor said. "I'm impressed. That's a big topic."

"Yep, it's big! Really big! Huge, in fact!" She flipped open her notebook to a fresh page and smiled brightly at them. "That's why I'm spending hours in here, reading—"

Taylor reached out to turn over the book Kelsi

had been reading. She read the title out loud: *The Essential Guide to Traveling and Living in Paris.* She smirked. "Uh-huh. That should help explain why Frenchmen decided to kick their king off the throne a couple of centuries ago."

Kelsi smiled sheepishly. "Okay, I admit that this isn't *exactly* on topic—"

"But you've suddenly developed a deep interest in the country of France," Gabriella said, a teasing light in her eyes. "I get it."

"I totally get it," Taylor said. "That Jean-Luc is so cute. And his accent is—" She paused, searching for the right word.

"Magnifique," Kelsi offered.

"Très magnifique," Gabriella said, laughing. "So, Kelsi, have you had a chance to talk to Jean-Luc yet?"

Kelsi's smile dimmed. "Not really."

"Why not?" Taylor asked. "Girl, you two are so right for each other! I mean, you love art and music and culture! You've been studying French since seventh grade! And what was the name of that music you played for the last talent show?"

"*L'Isle Joyeuse* by Claude Debussy," Kelsi said. "It's one of my favorites."

"Exactly! French!" Taylor threw up her hands to demonstrate that she had made her point. "You and Jean-Luc have so much in common. You're practically soul mates!" She paused and then added meaningfully, "You just have to talk to him."

Kelsi bit her lip and looked from Taylor to Gabriella. Then she blurted out, "But that's the problem! I can't! I think of things to say to him—but then when I see him, I can't even say hello!"

"You're just shy," Gabriella said soothingly. "And lots of guys like shy girls."

"Only if they notice you," Kelsi pointed out. "And face it, what chance do I have when Sharpay is obviously interested in him? She's been glued to his side ever since he got here. I mean, I know Principal Matsui asked her to show him around, but—"

"But now it's time for him to find his own way," Taylor said firmly. "I agree. And I think you need to help him do that, Kelsi."

"Don't worry so much about saying the right thing," Gabriella added. "Just start with hello and see what happens!"

"You're right. I'll try . . ." Kelsi said, but she didn't look convinced. She glanced at her watch. "Oh, I'm supposed to be in the music room right now, helping Mrs. Jones with arrangements for the spring concert. Thanks, guys. I'll see you later."

She scooped up her papers and scurried off.

As Gabriella and Taylor watched her go, Gabriella said, "I think we may have made Kelsi even more nervous by encouraging her to talk to Jean-Luc."

"Yeah, she seemed pretty eager to get out of here," Taylor said. "I was just trying to be a good friend. I know Jean-Luc would like Kelsi if she'd just put herself forward a little bit."

"Hmm . . ." Gabriella said, giving Taylor a knowing glance.

"What are you thinking, Gabriella?" Taylor asked. "Is it maybe what I'm thinking?"

Gabriella grinned mischievously. "I was just thinking that we are Kelsi's friends. And if a friend needs a little help, shouldn't we offer some?"

Taylor had already started nodding. "As in a little matchmaking help?"

"Great minds think alike," Gabriella said.

"Well, we'd better put our great minds to work," Taylor said. "Especially if Sharpay is after Jean-Luc, too!"

By lunchtime, Gabriella and Taylor had a plan, and they were ready to put it into action. They walked into the cafeteria and, as they got their food, quickly scoped out the tables. Troy, Chad, Jason, and Zeke were sitting at their usual table, halfway across the room. Fortunately, Sharpay had commandeered a spot only two tables away from them and was holding court with Jean-Luc, Ryan, and two of her Drama Club followers, Alicia Thomas and Charlotte Richards. Sharpay and Ryan were both wearing berets set at a jaunty angle.

Gabriella and Taylor walked over to Troy and Chad's table, carefully carrying their lunch trays.

"Hi, Gabriella!" Troy said. "You're just in time to help us guess what Jason's little sister made for his lunch."

"Yeah, she's decided she wants to combine her interest in science with her interest in cooking, so she's turned our kitchen into a laboratory," Jason said, shaking his head. "This is her latest experiment." He held up a plastic bag filled with what looked like murky green goop. "If you guess what it is, you get half."

"I keep telling you, you've got that backwards," Chad said. "I think the loser has to help you eat that.

"Sounds like a fun game," Gabriella said. "But actually, we can't join you guys today. We thought we'd sit with Jean-Luc, help him feel at home."

Chad slumped back in his seat, his arms folded across his chest. "Sure," he said, rather sulkily. "Go ahead. You'll have to fight through the crowds, though."

"We eat lunch together all the time," Taylor pointed out. "This is no big deal."

Troy looked at Gabriella, forcing a smile. "You're right," he said. "It's tough being a new kid. We'll catch up with you later."

"Thanks for understanding, Troy," Gabriella said softly.

As she and Taylor edged their way through the tables, she whispered to Taylor, "I hope Chad wasn't really upset."

Taylor sighed. "He's just a little jealous. But once he sees what we're doing, he'll understand." She stopped a few feet away from Sharpay's table and looked around the crowded cafeteria. Every table was packed with students, who were eating, talking, laughing, arguing.

Taylor smiled to herself as she scanned the room. Ever since Troy and Gabriella had shown East High how much fun it was to hang out with different people, the cafeteria had become a meeting place for all kinds of mixed groups. She saw hip-hop kids chatting with brainiacs, athletes engaged in earnest discussions with band kids, and a couple of techno geeks explaining computer setups to a few girls from the drill team.

But no matter how hard Taylor looked, she couldn't see the one person who was necessary for their plan to work.

She muttered to Gabriella, "You did tell Kelsi to meet us here, right?"

"Yes, she said she'd be here," Gabriella answered, "but that she might be a little late."

Taylor gave a brisk nod. "Good. That will give us time to set things up."

As they approached Sharpay's table, they could clearly hear her voice rising above the rest.

"I talked to Daddy last night, and he said he

thought it would be a fabulous idea to have our next family vacation in Paris!" she said.

Taylor glanced at Gabriella and rolled her eyes ever so slightly. Gabriella bit her lip to keep from grinning. It was one thing to have wealthy parents, the way Sharpay and Ryan did, but it was another thing to brag about it all the time. However, the students who liked to hang out with Sharpay never thought that her bragging was obnoxious; in fact, they were rather impressed by everything she experienced. Alicia and Charlotte were staring at Sharpay in wonder at the thought of her trip.

After a moment, Alicia managed to say, "Wow, a trip to Paris! That is so cool!"

"I know," Sharpay said smugly, readjusting the beret that she was wearing. "I've decided that I must prepare for this trip as seriously as I prepare for a major acting role. Everything I do—from what I wear to what I eat to the people I hang out with—has to be related to France! See?"

As Gabriella and Taylor sat down across from

Alicia and Charlotte, Sharpay began unpacking her lunch, placing each item on the table with a grand flourish. "Brie."

Charlotte wrinkled her nose. "What's that? It looks kind of funny."

"It's a very special and very delicious French cheese," Sharpay said. "A baguette . . ." She saw Alicia's puzzled expression and added, "That's the French name for a special kind of bread. And, of course, fruit."

She smiled warmly at Jean-Luc. "I don't suppose you've seen a meal like that since you left the Champs-Élysées!"

"Well, actually, I live in a suburb of Paris, so I don't get to the Champs-Élysées that often. Your lunch does look delicious, though," he said diplomatically. "But I love American food. Like this!" He picked up a hamburger from his tray and took a big bite.

"That smells great," Ryan said. He cast a longing look at Jean-Luc's burger and fries, then turned back to his own lunch, which was the same as Sharpay's. He nibbled a slice of apple as Jean-Luc ate three French fries at once.

At that moment, Gabriella spotted Kelsi and waved her over. Kelsi made her way through the crowd, but when she got to the table she hesitated, holding her brown lunch bag with both hands and looking down at the ground.

"Have a seat, Kelsi," Taylor said, quickly pushing the chair next to Jean-Luc with her foot so that it appeared right in front of Kelsi.

Kelsi jumped back as if the chair had attacked her, but then she gulped and sat down. As she opened up her lunch bag and began arraying her sandwich, soda, and chips on the table, Gabriella said brightly, "Jean-Luc, you remember Kelsi from homeroom, don't you?"

"Of course." He smiled at Kelsi warmly. She blushed, but managed to meet his eyes and give a small nod in return.

Well, that's something, Gabriella thought. Now we just need to get her to talk to him. . . .

"Kelsi, are you looking forward to the talent show?" she prodded.

"Yes," Kelsi whispered.

Taylor looked at Gabriella. Gabriella knew what that expression meant: what can we do to get this girl to flirt a little? She shrugged at Taylor.

"Kelsi loves French music," Taylor piped up to Jean-Luc. She turned back to her friend and added, "Tell me again what piece you played for the talent show last semester?"

"*L'Isle Joyeuse* by Claude Debussy," Kelsi said, her voice still barely audible.

Jean-Luc nodded, but he didn't seem too interested.

Gabriella and Taylor exchanged puzzled looks. They had thought Jean-Luc would be intrigued to know that Kelsi loved a French composer and that he would want to talk more with her.

"But I'm playing a piano sonata by Aaron Copland for this year's talent show," Kelsi added shyly.

"Really!" Jean-Luc turned toward Kelsi, his face brightening. "Aaron Copland is one of my favorite composers," he said. *"Rodeo! Billy the Kid!"*

Finally, a tiny smile appeared on Kelsi's face. "I love those songs, too," she said.

"So," he said, leaning toward her, "you play the piano?"

Bolstered by Jean-Luc's sudden interest, Kelsi lost all her self-consciousness. Her smile widened as her face began to glow.

"Yes," she began. "I love it! I would play the piano all day if I could!"

"That's wonderful," he said. "I love music as well, but I could never seem to master the keyboard, even after years of lessons. Now, string instruments, on the other hand—"

"Ow!" Ryan's gasp of pain interrupted Jean-Luc and made everyone at the table turn his way. His eyes watering, Ryan reached down to rub the ankle that Sharpay had just kicked. It had been a kick full of meaning, and Ryan had no problem figuring out what she was getting at. Quickly, he turned the subject back to where Sharpay always felt it belonged: her. "So," he said loudly, "what was that you were saying last night about our trip to Paris, sis?"

Sharpay placed her hand on Jean-Luc's arm. "I was just saying," she cooed, "that I can't wait to get the inside scoop from Jean-Luc about where we should go and what we should see!"

"Of course," Jean-Luc said politely. "I'd be glad to suggest some places. . . ."

As the conversation went on, Kelsi sighed and began eating her sandwich. Gabriella saw the look of disappointment on her friend's face and felt a surge of determination rise in her. Sharpay might be going to Paris, but Jean-Luc had to be shown that Kelsi was worth getting to know as well. And she could tell from the look on Taylor's face that she felt the same way.

CHAPTER
FOUR

The next afternoon, Troy and Chad were teaching Jean-Luc some key moves on the basketball court in Troy's backyard.

"All right, Jean-Luc, you've got the ball!" Troy called out. "Now just dribble toward the basket. That's it, you're doing awesome! Just keep going!"

Jean-Luc dashed across the court, his eyes narrowed in concentration as he tried to bounce the ball and run.

"Remember to watch out for defenders!" Chad

yelled. He quickly moved into Jean-Luc's way. "There are going to be guys trying to keep you from getting to the other end of the court, you know."

"*Oui*, I know," Jean-Luc panted as he took a few steps to the left to move around Chad.

But Chad saw where he was going and moved even faster. Jean-Luc moved to the right and Chad followed suit. Flustered, Jean-Luc turned sharply and headed for the side of the court, hoping to loop around Chad, but now Chad was bearing down on his right—

"Ha!" Chad snatched the ball in between bounces and darted toward the basket. He jumped and threw, and the ball slid through the net with a swish.

Jean-Luc stopped and leaned over with his hands on his knees, breathing hard. "This basketball is harder than it looks on TV," he commented. "Much harder."

Chad trotted back to where Jean-Luc was standing and patted him on the back. "Don't worry, man," he said cheerfully. "For someone who's only been playing for . . ." He checked his watch. ". . . twenty minutes or so, you're doing a phenomenal job."

Troy shot Chad a warning look. He was glad to see his friend warming up to Jean-Luc, but his improved mood seemed to be due to the fact that he was running rings around Jean-Luc on the basketball court.

"Let's take a water break," Troy suggested. "Then Jean-Luc can practice driving toward the basket *without* any interference." He gave Chad a meaningful look. Then he turned to Jean-Luc and said, "I think you just need to concentrate on dribbling so you can learn how the move feels. If you try to learn too many things at once, you'll just get confused."

"That sounds good to me," Jean-Luc said gratefully as he took a gulp from his water bottle. He nodded at Chad and added, "You are an excellent player, Chad. I'm glad I'm going up against you, because I am sure I will learn a lot."

Troy was amused to see Chad's mouth drop

open at the sincerity in Jean-Luc's voice. "Well, uh, thanks," Chad muttered. "You're catching on fast. Really."

"Yeah," Troy agreed. "For someone who hasn't played much, you seem to have a natural feel for the game."

Jean-Luc grinned. "Thank you, but I can tell I have much to learn."

"So, let's get started!" Troy said.

Ninety minutes later, the three boys were the best of friends. They were swigging water and replaying their best moves from the practice session when Gabriella and Taylor walked into the backyard.

"Hi, guys," Gabriella said. "Troy, your mom told us we would find you here."

"Not that it was much of a surprise," Taylor added drily. "So there's no basketball practice today, and you decide to spend your free afternoon playing basketball?"

"What can I say?" Chad grinned. "We love the sport. And . . ." He pointed to her book bag, which looked like it was about to burst open. "What have you and Gabriella been doing?"

"Okay, okay," Taylor said defensively. "I admit it, we were at the city library."

"Of course you were," Troy said, casting a teasing look in Gabriella's direction. "On a beautiful afternoon like this, where else would you want to be except—"

"Hiding in the stacks and researching the Spanish colonial history of New Mexico," Gabriella finished, laughing. "But at least we managed to come up for air long enough to see if you guys wanted to go get some ice cream."

"After this workout, I'm ready for three scoops," Chad declared.

The back gate opened then, and Sharpay barged into the Boltons' backyard. When she saw Jean-Luc, she beamed.

"Jean-Luc, there you are!" she cried.

"She's hunted you down, man," Chad muttered to Jean-Luc. "Run! I'll cover for you!"

But Jean-Luc just smiled politely and nodded

to Sharpay. "Hello, Sharpay," he said. "Nice to see you." There was just the slightest pause before he added, "Again."

"I hope you didn't forget our date this evening," she said coyly.

Gabriella looked over at Taylor, surprised. Sharpay was dating Jean-Luc?

Jean-Luc looked confused at first, then his face cleared. "Oh, of course, this is Wednesday!" he said. "I am sorry. I did forget about the dinner with your family."

Gabriella breathed a sigh of relief. Not a date, then. Not really.

"But I need to change," Jean-Luc said, looking down at himself. "I can't meet your parents like this!"

"Don't worry, I'll drive you by your hotel so you can shower and change," Sharpay said. She batted her eyes a bit. "You know, Mother and Daddy just can't wait to meet *you*!"

Jean-Luc nodded, but Gabriella thought she could see his easy smile dim just a bit. He looked even more dismayed when Sharpay went on to say, "And after dinner, I'd love to get your opinion about which new song I should perform at the talent show!"

Taylor tilted her head, suddenly alert. "I thought you had already picked out what you were going to perform," she said suspiciously.

"Oh, I changed my mind," Sharpay said breezily. "I thought I'd sing something a little more sophisticated, a little more . . . French." She smiled up at Jean-Luc. "In honor of you."

He cleared his throat. "Ah, well, that's very nice, but you really don't have to do that," he began, stammering a little.

"Nonsense! I want to! And I want you to listen to me sing all the songs I'm considering. I've narrowed it down to twelve—"

Jean-Luc paled.

"Come on, Sharpay, we're supposed to be *welcoming* Jean-Luc, not torturing him while he's here!" Chad said. "Can't he have just a little fun?"

"We are going to have fun!" Sharpay said huffily. "After Jean-Luc helps me choose my song, we're going to hang out in our new screening room! Daddy just had a state-of-the-art projection system put in, and I rented some movies set in Paris. I thought that watching those would be a great way to get in the mood for our trip."

"Oh, so your parents and Ryan will be watching the movies, too?" Jean-Luc asked hopefully. "Since you are planning a family vacation?"

But Sharpay shook her head. "In my family, I'm the one in charge of making our vacations memorable, so I thought I'd do all the advance research on my own," she said as she linked her arm through his. "It will be just me and you!"

As she pulled Jean-Luc toward her car, she called back over her shoulder, "*Au revoir*, fellow Wildcats! And *à bientôt!*"

There was a long silence after she left. Then Gabriella turned to Troy. "See, this is what we were talking about!" she said. "Jean-Luc only has two weeks here, and Sharpay is going to make sure that she monopolizes him the whole time!"

"Poor guy," Chad said, shaking his head.

"You're exactly right, Chad," Taylor said.

Chad furrowed his brow suspiciously. Taylor almost never said he was *exactly* right!

"You and Troy need to help us get Jean-Luc together with Kelsi," Taylor went on.

Chad shook his head as hard as he could. "Uh-uh, no way, forget it," he said.

"But why not?" Gabriella asked sweetly. "They have so much in common, I know they would like each other, it would be so easy to—"

She stopped herself midsentence. Both Chad and Troy were looking at her with identical expressions of horror. "What's wrong with doing a little matchmaking?" she finished.

"It's not wrong," Chad said. "It's just . . ."

Troy stepped in and said firmly, "It's just that guys don't do that kind of thing."

"Exactly!" Chad said. "And not only that, but

you wouldn't want us to try! I mean, we'd do it all wrong and mess everything up."

Troy nodded quickly. "That's right. Guys just don't have the knack."

"And how do you know that, exactly?" Taylor asked, crossing her arms and giving them a cool look. "Given that, according to your own testimony, you've never even tried?"

Chad had to exert all his self-control not to make a face. He hated it when Taylor started sounding like a lawyer, especially when he was the one on trial! "Well, we just know," he said, trying to bluff his way out of the conversation.

Taylor narrowed her eyes in a way that meant she wasn't buying his lame excuse.

"That's okay," Gabriella said. "Never mind."

Troy and Chad turned to look at her in surprise. "Really?" Troy said.

She smiled. "You made a good point. And I wouldn't want you to help us if you feel uncomfortable. Taylor and I will figure out another way to get Kelsi and Jean-Luc together."

"Great!" Troy said with relief. "I knew you'd understand."

Taylor frowned. She wasn't ready to give up so easily. In fact, she was a little surprised that Gabriella was.

"And I can understand that you guys wouldn't want to get in Sharpay's way," Gabriella continued. "Sometimes she's so single-minded, she's a little scary!"

"What are you talking about?" Chad puffed out his chest. "We're not afraid of Sharpay!"

Troy nodded. "And even if we were—"

"Which we're not!" Chad insisted.

"Right." Troy nodded again. "We're not, but even if we were, what does that have to do with anything?"

Gabriella shrugged, her face the picture of innocence. "Just that Sharpay clearly wants to spend every free moment with Jean-Luc."

"I wouldn't wish that fate on anybody!" Chad said seriously.

"And he's such a good guy," Troy said. "Did you know he's a really big basketball fan?"

Taylor started to grin when she realized what Gabriella was doing, but she bit her smile back just in time. Instead, she clucked sadly and said, "Yeah, I heard him talking about how impressed he was with the Wildcats. But I guess he won't have many stories to tell when he gets back to Paris. Not if he spends all his time with Sharpay. Or, rather, all his stories will be about Sharpay."

"If only we could get him out of Sharpay's clutches," Gabriella said wistfully. "You know, give him time to meet other people."

There was a long silence. Then Troy snapped his fingers. "I have an idea!" he said. "I bet if we worked together, we could keep Sharpay away from Jean-Luc. And if he's busy with other friends, she can't take up all his time, right?"

Gabriella tried not to laugh as Chad nodded eagerly and said, "That's the least we can do for a buddy."

"I think that's a great idea," Gabriella said, smiling at Troy and Chad. "Hey, I thought we were going for ice cream?"

"You're right. Wait here while we change," Troy said.

As Troy and Chad ran inside, Taylor turned to Gabriella and started laughing. "I have to hand it to you," she said. "When it comes to scheming, you're getting to be as good as Sharpay!"

CHAPTER FIVE

On Friday after lunch, Kelsi headed to the music room during her free period. It was empty, as usual. She flopped down on the piano bench and closed her eyes for a few minutes, enjoying the chance to be alone. The day was only half over, and it had already been stressful beyond belief! First, there was homeroom. In the past, Kelsi had dreaded this period. She used to take a seat in the back row and keep her head down as everyone else joked around and teased each other, scared that someone would actually say something to her—or even worse, that she would have to say something back! But ever since last year's musical, when Troy and Gabriella had taken the school by storm, Kelsi had started coming out of her shell. And after she had, she'd become friends with the other Wildcats and found herself actually looking forward to homeroom.

But that was BJL: Before Jean-Luc.

Kelsi wanted to talk to him, she really did. But for some reason, every time she tried to think of something to say—even when she planned something out ahead of time—she found herself tongue-tied. And it was so frustrating because they had so many things in common!

France, for example. Jean-Luc lived there. And she had always wanted to visit! Surely that was enough of a bond right there? Then Kelsi remembered how Sharpay had grabbed all of his attention yesterday in the cafeteria by boasting about her family trip to Paris, and her spirits sank. After all, Kelsi's parents weren't going to take a vacation to Paris anytime soon. Kelsi knew she'd probably have to wait until she was in college and doing her junior year abroad before she set foot on the Champs-Élysées.

But then there was the French language. Jean-Luc spoke it. She was studying it. It should be easy to get a conversation started. Unfortunately, Kelsi realized that she was shy in not just one but *two* languages! She played a few sad little notes at this thought and tried to come up with something else they had in common.

Well, there was the fact that he loved the composer Aaron Copland, of course. And then there was the moment yesterday in history class when he had spoken so eloquently about the brilliance of America's Founding Fathers, not knowing that Kelsi secretly loved reading biographies of Thomas Jefferson. And that morning in homeroom, he had casually mentioned that he planned to visit Bali someday, which had always been number one on

Kelsi's list of places to visit before she turned thirty. . . .

Here they were, practically soul mates, and Jean-Luc would never know because she was too nervous to say one single word to him. It was a tragedy. Kelsi sat and brooded about that for a few minutes, then decided that she couldn't stand being in a black mood all day. So she placed her hands on the piano keys and began to play scales to warm up. She knew that playing the piano would cheer her up.

But her fingers seemed to find only the scales in minor keys; almost without noticing, she began playing a song that sounded plaintive and mournful. It only took a few minutes for Kelsi to realize that she felt even worse than she had when she walked into the music room, which had never happened before.

She shook her head slightly and opened up the music she would be playing for the competition. Her fingers began moving over the keys, and the rhythm of the song took over. Soon she had forgotten everything except the music that was filling the room.

While Kelsi played the piano, trying to cheer herself up, Gabriella and Taylor were going over their supersneaky plan one last time.

"Okay, Jean-Luc has third-period history, then he has fourth-period study hall," Gabriella hissed to Taylor. "That means he's heading from Ms. Garrison's class down the hall to the north stairway, which he'll take—"

"To the first floor, at which point he'll turn left to go to the library," Taylor finished. "Gotcha."

Gabriella grinned as Taylor held up her hand for a high five. "Right. And Sharpay is also heading for the library, where I'm sure she plans to corner Jean-Luc and ask him to come over to her house to help her practice her song again. I'll intercept Jean-Luc. You need to worry about Sharpay."

"No problem." Taylor's dark eyes were alight with mischief. "I am all over that girl. She won't know what hit her!"

They high-fived each other one more time for luck, then headed out on their separate missions.

Taylor didn't have any problem spotting Sharpay. Her bright yellow dress with its wide, flounced skirt in the style of the 1950s stood out like a giant sunflower among the rest of the students, who were mainly wearing jeans and T-shirts. Even Alicia and Charlotte, Sharpay's Drama Club followers, seemed to fade a little when they stood next to her.

Taylor didn't have any trouble hearing Sharpay, either. Even over the commotion in the hallway, Sharpay's voice rang out. "I'm going to the library to study for a while," she was saying. "That French test next week is going to be terrible, I just know it. Fortunately"—she gave Alicia and Charlotte a coy smile—"I'm going to have some expert tutoring help."

Taylor seethed. Trust Sharpay to hint to everyone that she and Jean-Luc were an item—even if he didn't know it yet!

Sharpay waved her fingers at the Drama Club girls and called out, "Toodles!" before barreling down the hall toward the stairs. Taylor waited until the last second, then stepped out in front of her.

"Aah!" Sharpay yelled. "Watch where you're going, Taylor! I almost broke a heel!"

"Oh, no!" Taylor's eyes widened in what looked like sympathy. "That would *truly* be a disaster."

"Exactly. I chose my outfit very carefully this morning." Sharpay frowned as she stared at her foot, turning it this way and that to make sure her shoe wasn't damaged. "It's important that I look my absolute best."

"Oh, I know," Taylor said, doing her best to sound impressed. "I heard."

"You did?" Sharpay looked confused. "What did you hear?"

"That Ms. Darbus is so excited about the new song you're doing for the talent show that she's having the stage crew design a special backdrop featuring a Paris street scene," Taylor said smoothly.

She chose not to mention that the special backdrop had been her idea, or that Gabriella had mentioned it to Ms. Darbus, who had flung her hands in the air and cried *"Marveilleux!"* Then she dashed to her filing cabinet to see if she had any suitable designs tucked away.

"Ms. Darbus is even giving out extra detentions to make sure it gets done on time. Fair warning: don't let your cell phone go off in homeroom this week!" Taylor laughed as she said this. Ms. Darbus was known for having students serve their detention in the theater, where they worked as part of the stage crew. But Sharpay's mind was clearly on other things. Her eyes were narrowed in thought.

"I have a darling outfit, all blue and silver spangles," she said out loud. "Mother's dressmaker whipped up something based on a famous cabaret singer who lived in Paris in the 1920s. . . ."

"Blue and silver?" Taylor looked troubled.

"But I think the backdrop is going to be mostly blue. When you stand in front of it, you'll—"

"*Blend in!*" Sharpay cried out, putting a hand to her forehead. She looked as though she might faint.

"What a shame," Taylor said, throwing a little fuel on the fire. "Especially after you put in all that work making sure that you would stand out."

Sharpay's chin lifted defiantly. "And I still will!" she said. "I just have to go talk to Ms. Darbus now!"

As Sharpay rushed down the hall in the direction she'd just come from, Taylor smiled. Now Gabriella just had to do her job, and their plan would be set in motion.

"Thank you for showing me around the school," Jean-Luc said to Gabriella. "It's very nice of you. But, if I may ask, where exactly is this historical object you want me to see? We seem to have been walking for some time, and I do need to go to the library during my free period. . . ."

"Don't worry, we're almost there." Gabriella

gave him a smiling glance over her shoulder as she led him down the hall. Finally, she stopped in front of a glass case filled with trophies. The larger and more impressive ones were at the front of the case, but Gabriella pointed to a small, tarnished object in the back corner. "There, you see that? That was the very first basketball trophy ever won by East High, way back when the school was in another building."

"Ah." Jean-Luc leaned forward and dutifully peered at the tiny basketball player leaping atop the trophy. "Very . . . um . . . interesting."

Gabriella nodded and held her breath while listening as hard as she could. Nothing but silence in the hallway. Gabriella started feeling anxious. Surely she and Taylor had gotten the times correct. They had organized their schedules precisely. Their plan couldn't go wrong now. . . .

Then, just as planned, the sound of piano music drifted into the corridor.

And just as Gabriella had expected, the music

caught Jean-Luc's ear. He turned around to scan the hall.

"Where is that music coming from?" he asked.

"The music room," Gabriella said. She opened her eyes wide in mock surprise. "Hasn't anyone shown you the music room yet? Well, I'm certainly glad I brought you over to this part of the school! Here, let's see if we can just poke our heads in for a minute."

Half an hour later, Jean-Luc had forgotten that he had planned to go to the library to study for an algebra test. His plan to stop at the cafeteria and pick up a snack had completely slipped his mind as well. And the fact that Gabriella had made some excuse and left twenty-five minutes ago had gone completely unnoticed.

Instead, he was totally focused on watching Kelsi as she played another song for him. And this song, she had explained shyly, was one that she had actually written herself. Jean-Luc was filled with admiration for her talent. As he watched her intense concentration—so focused that she didn't even blink when a brown curl fell into her eyes—he found himself wishing he hadn't allowed himself to be roped into spending so much time with Sharpay. Time that he could have been spending with . . . Kelsi.

Kelsi finished the song and glanced over at him. "That's it," she said. "It's not really finished yet. I know I need to work on it some more, it's just something I've been playing around with and I know it's not really good yet—"

Jean-Luc held up his hand to stop her. "It's wonderful," he said. "I wish I could write something half as good."

Kelsi gave him a relieved smile. "Thanks." Her brow furrowed. "But didn't you say that you play an instrument? I thought that yesterday at lunch . . ."

"Oh, yes, well." Jean-Luc shrugged modestly. "My mother insisted. And since I couldn't seem to grasp the piano, I moved on to the cello." He nodded toward a corner of the room where the instrument stood.

Kelsi looked amazed—far more amazed, Jean-Luc thought, than his admission warranted. Then she said, "That's incredible! I was just thinking last night that this song would sound so much better if it were a duet for piano and cello!"

Suddenly, any memory that Jean-Luc had of agreeing to go to the Lava Springs Country Club with Sharpay vanished from his mind. He smiled warmly at Kelsi.

"I think your idea is very good," he said as he walked across the room to take the cello from its stand. "In fact, why don't we try it right now?"

CHAPTER SIX

Kelsi couldn't believe how well she and Jean-Luc had hit it off as they practiced playing the music she had written. They had been completely absorbed in creating a cello part that would complement the piano. When Kelsi hit a roadblock, Jean-Luc had an inventive solution; when Jean-Luc ran into difficulty with a rapid arpeggio, she rewrote that section of the score and found that the new version was even better than the old. Kelsi was used to working alone when she composed music. If anyone had asked her before, she would have said she liked it that way. But now she was learning that she also liked collaboration . . . at least with Jean-Luc.

When they'd finished rehearsing, they walked into the hall, still chatting eagerly. Kelsi was feeling very happy.

"It is almost the weekend, is it not?" Jean-Luc said. "What do you normally do on your free days?"

"Well, I—" she began.

"Jean-Luc, there you are!" Sharpay came dashing around the corner and skidded to a stop in front of them. "I've been looking all over for you!"

"Oh?" Jean-Luc did not sound particularly thrilled at this news. "Why is that?"

"I wanted to tell you about the fabulous Parisian backdrop that Ms. Darbus is creating for my talent show number," she said. "And I wanted to invite you to the country club dance on Saturday night. The theme is 'Hurray for

Hollywood'! Everyone is going to dress up as their favorite movie character." She paused, then added coyly, "I'm going to go as the character Leslie Caron played in *An American in Paris*. You can go as her dance partner, Gene Kelly. I've put together the perfect costume for you."

"Well, that's very nice of you," Jean-Luc said. He glanced uneasily from Kelsi to Sharpay. "But, actually, I was about to make other plans—"

"But you haven't yet, so your schedule is still free," Sharpay cried happily. "How perfect! We'll pick you up at seven. Toodles!"

As she flounced off, Jean-Luc shrugged apologetically. "I was hoping we could do something together. Perhaps in the afternoon or on Sunday?"

"Sure," Kelsi said, trying not to sound too eager. "Let me give you my number."

But, as it turned out, Sharpay had filled up every minute of Jean-Luc's weekend with a picnic in the park, a long bike ride, a trip to the zoo, and a prolonged game of Scrabble in her family's game room. All too soon it was Monday morning, and Kelsi realized sadly that Jean-Luc was only going to be at East High for another week. Sharpay was sure to find even more reasons to monopolize his attention as the time got shorter and shorter.

Kelsi was normally a very cheerful person, but she was looking pretty glum when she ran into Gabriella by her locker that morning.

"Hey, what's up?" Gabriella asked. "Is everything okay? You look like you just got some bad news."

"Oh, no, everything's fine," Kelsi said, but she said it with such a heavy sigh that Gabriella took her arm and pulled her aside.

"Come on, Kelsi, what's wrong?" she asked.

"It's Jean-Luc," Kelsi said. "And Sharpay."

As Gabriella listened to Kelsi's story, she was thinking hard. When Kelsi finished, she said, "Don't worry. I'm going to figure out a way to make sure you and Jean-Luc get to spend some time together."

"Really?" Kelsi wanted to believe her, but she was skeptical. "How?"

"You leave that to me," Gabriella said with determination. "Just meet me at the gym after school for basketball practice. I'll take it from there."

That afternoon, Jean-Luc was suited up and ready to go as soon as basketball practice started. As he jogged up and down the court, Zeke and Jason looked at him in surprise, then at each other, then at Troy.

"What's up, cap?" Zeke said. "Did we get a new teammate overnight?"

Jason winced as Jean-Luc picked up a basketball and started dribbling. He only managed three bounces before losing the ball and chasing it across the floor.

"Don't worry, guys," Troy said, laughing. "Jean-Luc just wants to learn about the game, so Chad and I have been coaching him a little bit. I thought it might be fun for him to practice with the team. It would be great if you could help him out a little. You know, make him feel at home."

"Sure, no problem," Jason said.

Zeke nodded. "We'll show him how to play basketball Wildcat-style!"

They jogged over to Jean-Luc. "Hey, want some help?" Zeke asked.

"Thanks," Jean-Luc said gratefully. "I can bounce the ball when I'm standing still, but when I try to move—"

He demonstrated. The ball went flying again.

Zeke nodded wisely. "That's always the problem," he said. "Here, let me show you a little trick. . . ."

Zeke palmed the ball, then Jean-Luc tried to copy what he was doing. Their attention was so focused that they didn't notice Sharpay as she dashed through the door and over to the bleachers, teetering on her high heels. By the time she had seated herself next to Alicia and Charlotte, Coach Bolton was motioning for the team to gather around him.

"Everybody's been doing a great job executing our plays," he said. "But West High is always a tough opponent. They won't let up until the final buzzer, so you guys need to be in great shape. Let's start with some conditioning. Everybody line up for wind sprints."

Amid good-natured groans, the players began moving toward one end of the court. Jean-Luc went with them, although more slowly, since he was concentrating on bouncing the ball with every step.

"You're looking good, Jean-Luc!" Sharpay called out from the stands. "You're looking *formidable*, as a matter of fact!"

Alicia and Charlotte clapped appreciatively and cheered their encouragement.

Jean-Luc couldn't help looking at them, but he glanced away quickly. When he caught Troy's eye, he gave a sheepish shrug. "I did not ask them to come to practice," he said, looking worried.

Troy laughed and clapped him on the back. "Don't worry. I know Sharpay very well. She does exactly what she wants to do. Always."

Jean-Luc looked relieved. Then Sharpay organized her mini-Drama Club into chanting, "Jean-Luc! Jean-Luc! Jean-Luc!" He turned bright red.

Chad jostled Jean-Luc's elbow as they lined up at the end of the court. "Dude, nice work! You've got your own private cheering section."

Jean-Luc turned even redder. "I did not *ask*—" he began again.

"Hey, I'm just teasing you," Chad said quickly. "I know you didn't want her to come to practice and yell your name every five minutes and completely embarrass you in front of the entire team—"

Troy cleared his throat and shot Chad a stern look. "What Chad means," he said, "is that we all know what Sharpay is like."

"Right," Jason chimed in. "And we wouldn't wish her on, well, anybody."

"Hey," Zeke said in protest. "Sharpay's not all that bad. . . ."

"Zeke, please," Chad said, shooting his team-mate a serious look. "You're delusional." Turning back to Jean-Luc, he continued, "I'm sorry I teased you about her, Jean-Luc. Really. I feel your pain."

"Thank you, *mon ami*," Jean-Luc said.

At that moment, Coach Bolton clapped his hands and yelled, "Thirty sprints, guys! Let's go!"

"Perhaps," Jean-Luc added just before they started racing back and forth across the gym, "she will get bored with us all and leave."

But Sharpay did not get bored. Well, she *did* get bored with all the basketball. She could only stand to watch boys bouncing a ball, throwing a ball, catching a ball for so long . . . even when the boys were Troy and Jean-Luc.

But she would never get tired of jumping up and down, cheering, dancing in the stands, and generally making sure that everyone was looking at her every minute.

After twenty minutes, however, she could feel that people's attention had drifted away. She looked around. The crowd had filled out a little. She spotted Gabriella, Taylor, and Kelsi, who had taken seats a few feet away in the second row. She recognized several boys whom she was sure had crushes on her sitting near the top of the bleachers. She was pleased to see a large group of Drama Club students—her biggest fans—sitting nearby. All in all, a pretty good crowd—except that something was wrong. Very wrong.

All heads had turned, ever so slightly, away from her and toward the gym doors.

She squinted. What in the world could be more fascinating than her? When she caught sight of the problem, she pressed her lips together with annoyance. That silly furry mascot again. Today he was cavorting along the sidelines, reaching out to shake people's hands, trying to get the girl with the unfortunate baggy gray sweatshirt to get up and dance, and pretending to play pranks on the cheerleaders, who were giggling over his antics.

It's all so childish, Sharpay thought, fuming. She couldn't understand why people found this creature so entertaining.

She crossed her arms and scowled at the mascot. As if he could feel her irritation, he turned to look in her direction. And then, before she knew it, he was cartwheeling toward her! He was climbing into the bleachers! He was waggling his hips and shaking his finger in her face, as if to scold her for her grumpy attitude!

This moth-eaten ball of fur was actually making fun of her! She simply couldn't believe it.

A wave of laughter rippled through the gym. Sharpay felt her face get hot. That's it! she thought, standing up. This has gone far enough! "I suppose you think you're very funny," she snapped.

The mascot nodded his head vigorously. Behind her, Sharpay could hear another chorus of giggles.

"Well, let me tell you something," she went on. "What you're doing is nothing but mime. And nobody likes mimes. Nobody!"

His head drooped. His shoulders sank. Every line of his body expressed dejection at this statement.

"Hey, give him a break, Sharpay," some guy yelled out.

"Yeah, he's only doing his job," someone else said.

She tossed her head. "Then why don't you do it," she hissed at the mascot, "down on the sidelines where you belong."

Wiley the Wildcat put his hands to his head, as if shocked by her anger, then turned to the crowd and gave an elaborate shrug.

From somewhere to her left, Sharpay heard something shocking. She heard faint booing.

She stiffened. Someone dared to "boo" her? Sharpay Evans? Because of this . . . this *nobody*?

"Who are you, anyway?" she asked.

That's when Wiley the Wildcat pulled his head off—and revealed Ryan's sweaty face.

Sharpay's mouth dropped open. Her eyes widened with shock. For one brief second, she was too flabbergasted to say a word.

Ryan smiled weakly. Maybe she wasn't really mad, maybe he would get away with this, maybe everything would actually be all right—

Then Sharpay found her voice. "Ryan!" she shrieked. "What do you think you're *doing*?"

Ryan had known that he was taking a risk when he offered to stand in as Wiley the Wildcat until Andrew's ankle healed. First, he hadn't cleared it with Sharpay before agreeing to take the job. Second, he hadn't informed Sharpay *after* he had agreed. And third—

Well, the third and final risk was that he would be good, really good. And even though he couldn't imagine that Sharpay would ever want to climb inside a musty mascot suit to perform for a crowd—especially since the suit would hide her face and was not at all flattering—she still hated to be upstaged by anyone. Even a super-sized plush animal.

That was quite clear when she had yelled at him in front of everyone. He had very briefly considered answering her question. What I think I'm doing, he would have said, is acting like a star!

But then, just in the nick of time, he had regained his senses. "Just having some fun, sis," he answered, and then jammed on the mascot head. He raced back down the bleachers to the sidelines. Now he gave a mental shrug and did three fast backflips in a row, just to clear his mind. He couldn't worry about Sharpay right now. After all, he had work to do. At that moment, Andrew slowly limped into the gym on crutches. Ryan bounded over to meet him.

"Hey, Andrew!" he called out as he took off the mascot head. His face was shining with happiness. "I wish you were here ten minutes ago! You should have seen me work the crowd. I followed your directions exactly, and it worked like a charm—"

"That's great, Evans, but don't get too comfortable," Andrew snarled. "Remember, that mascot job is *mine*! I won it fair and square! So don't think you can use my little accident as a way to take over from me—"

"No, no, of course not," Ryan said, making his voice as calm as he could. Fortunately, he had had a lot of experience soothing temperamental artists, he thought. "After all, *you're* the mascot master," he went on. "I'm just a humble apprentice, hoping to learn a few things before it's time for me to step out of the suit for good."

"Hmmph," Andrew grunted. "Well, you do have a lot to learn, but you're working hard at it. I can see that."

"Thanks, Andrew," Ryan said, gushing just a bit. "I'm giving this job everything I have! I don't want to let anyone down when it's time for the big game! I want to do so well that the crowd thinks that it's you here inside this suit!"

A fraction of a second too late, Ryan realized that he had overstepped his bounds.

Andrew's face darkened. "Let's get one thing straight," he said between gritted teeth. "No one will *ever* mistake you for me!"

"No, of course not," Ryan said, backtracking quickly. "I didn't mean—"

"Take that backflip series you just did," Andrew went on, not listening. "Sloppiest thing I've seen in years!"

Ryan bit his lip to keep from arguing. He'd been taking dance and movement classes since he was three years old, and he knew his backflips came very close to perfection. He forced himself to sound humble, however, as he said, "Sorry, Andrew. I tried to do it exactly the way you said—"

"Did I say to put civilians in danger by starting too close to the front row?" Andrew shouted. "Did I say to not check the perimeter before you started? Did I say to do anything without me here, ready to lead you through it?"

Ryan held on to his temper with effort. "I said

I was sorry," he muttered. What's with this guy? he thought. Even Sharpay doesn't sound like a Marine drill sergeant during rehearsals!

Well, actually . . . His mind flashed back to their last rehearsal for the talent show. Sharpay *had* been a little harsh when he had forgotten the step-ball-change in the middle of that last section. In fact, now that he thought about it, she had yelled so loud that his ears had been ringing until he went to bed. . . .

"Evans! Do you hear me?" Andrew moved forward a few inches with his crutches so he was standing nose to nose with Ryan.

Of course I hear you, Ryan thought bitterly. So does everyone else in the gym.

Out loud, he just said, "Yes, Andrew."

"Good. Because I am going to teach you everything I know about being a mascot," Andrew barked. "You are *not* going to ruin the name and reputation of Wiley the Wildcat with your performance! Is that understood?"

Ryan opened his mouth to answer, but before

he could utter a word, a cool, amused voice from behind him said, "Oh, please. You don't honestly think that what you do is a real performance, do you?"

He turned to see Sharpay looking down her nose at him and the furry head he held in his arms. "Of course," he said defensively. "After all, it involves dance moves—"

"And acting," Andrew chimed in.

"And mime," Ryan said.

"And audience involvement," Andrew finished up.

"It's not exactly art," Sharpay sniffed. "After all, you are dressed up like a cartoon character."

Ryan felt a surge of anger. He couldn't believe that she was dissing his new job as the stand-in mascot! Which was, actually, a very, very hard job, as he was quickly learning.

He lifted his chin defiantly. "Oh, yeah? Well, I'm going to prove to you that working as a mascot is just as artistic as singing some silly song onstage!"

"Yeah!" Andrew said defiantly. "And I'm going to help him!"

Ryan and Andrew nodded to each other, the picture of solidarity.

"You let me know when you've figured out how to prove that point," Sharpay said, curling her lip. "In the meantime—" She leaned in a little closer to emphasize her point, "don't ever make fun of me in front of a crowd again!"

Despite their newfound courage, Ryan and Andrew were too cowed by Sharpay's display to reply. She nodded, satisfied at their reaction, and flounced off.

Ryan and Andrew watched her go in silence. Then, once she had safely left the gym, Andrew turned to Ryan. "Did you mean what you said to your sister about proving that being a mascot is an art?"

"Of course," Ryan said. "I admit, I didn't realize how hard it was going to be at first, either."

Andrew nodded solemnly. "No one does

unless they've walked a mile in my costume," he said. "Or done a dozen backflips in it."

Ryan frowned slightly. "The question is, how can I prove it to Sharpay?"

A slight smile appeared on Andrew's face for the first time. "I have an idea about that," he said mischievously. "But first I need to get you in shape. Are you ready to train more intensely than you've ever trained in your life?"

Ryan gulped. There was a fanatical light in Andrew's eyes that told him that if he said yes, the next few days were not going to be fun. Then he remembered how Sharpay had sneered at him, and he nodded. "Yes," he said, "I am."

"Outstanding." Andrew pointed to a spot on the far side of the gym, away from the crowd, away from the basketball players, away from everybody. "I want to see you practicing backflips for the next half hour! And remember—by taking on this challenge, you're going to be defending the pride of mascots everywhere!"

Ryan nodded. "Got it," he said with determination. And he put on his furry head and started to work.

By the time the practice ended, Jean-Luc had learned to dribble the ball with consistency, if not confidence. He had successfully passed the ball a half-dozen times. And he had actually made a basket!

Jean-Luc was beaming as the team gathered in a circle, put their hands together, and then raised their arms, yelling, "Wildcats!"

As he walked toward the locker room, he saw Kelsi sitting with Gabriella and Taylor.

"Hi, Kelsi!" he called out. "Are you finished practicing for the day?"

Kelsi bit her lip, embarrassed. "Um, actually, I thought I'd take the afternoon off," she said. After all, she knew her piano piece so well she could play it backwards. And wasn't it just as important to spend quality time with her good friends, Gabriella and Taylor? And show support for Troy, Chad, Zeke, and Jason? And incidentally give herself the opportunity to watch Jean-Luc in action?

"Great idea," he said. "I, too, would like to take the rest of the afternoon off. Maybe we could go to the ice cream parlor that I have heard serves quite enormous ice-cream sundaes?"

Kelsi didn't have to turn her head to know that Gabriella and Taylor were exchanging pleased glances at this. Flustered, she said, "That um . . . sounds wonderful."

"Jean-Luc, Jean-Luc!" Sharpay's voice cut across Kelsi's as she clambered down the bleachers. Kelsi wondered briefly if Sharpay would make it down safely in her three-inch heels, but she only tripped a bit as she got to the floor. And then she used her stumble as an excuse to clutch Jean-Luc's arm. "You are doing a fantastic job learning basketball. Really, *très commendable!*"

Jean-Luc's smile looked a little forced, but he merely said, "Thank you. I have good coaches." He gestured toward Troy and Chad, who had walked over to join them.

"Oh, of course." Sharpay barely glanced at them before turning all her attention back to Jean-Luc. "Now, I know you want to shower and change, so I'll just pull my car in front of the gym to pick you up, okay?"

"Um . . ." Jean-Luc seemed confused.

"You do remember you promised to listen to me sing my new competition song this afternoon, don't you?" Sharpay went on sweetly.

Jean-Luc looked trapped. "Yes, of course, but I did not think that was today . . ." he began.

"Don't be silly, of course it's today," Sharpay said with a tinkling laugh. "After all, we only have a few days left until the competition! And if this song isn't just right and I have to choose another song, I'll need every minute to rehearse!" She gave him a coy glance from beneath her eyelashes. "You know I picked a French song in honor of you. You wouldn't want to keep me from doing my very best, would you?" Her voice turned steely. "And you *did* promise."

Kelsi caught her breath, outraged at how

completely shameless Sharpay was. Surely Jean-Luc wouldn't fall for a ploy as obvious as this. . . .

Then she looked over at him. His shoulders were slumped and his smile was gone, but he nodded. "You are right, I promised," he said. "Very well. I'll meet you in a few minutes."

Sharpay tossed her head and flashed a triumphant smile. "Fabulous!" she said. As she walked away, she turned to wave at Kelsi and her friends. "Toodles!"

Once she was gone, Jean-Luc said to Kelsi, "I am sorry. I forgot that I told Sharpay I would help her."

"Of course," Kelsi said, trying her best to sound bright and carefree. "I know how important it is to have someone help you rehearse."

"Perhaps we could have ice cream another time," he suggested.

"Absolutely," she said. This time she put an extra lilt in her voice, just so everyone would know that she was totally fine with being overshadowed by Sharpay. Again.

He nodded, looking relieved, and jogged off toward the locker room.

Kelsi met Gabriella's gaze. As she had suspected, Gabriella's eyes were filled with sympathy. But Kelsi didn't want her friend's sympathy; she wanted Jean-Luc to spend time with her, not Sharpay. And as long as she was up against East High's biggest drama queen, she knew the odds were not in her favor.

"I cannot believe Sharpay," Taylor said, fuming. "If you looked up the word 'pushy' in a dictionary, you'd see a picture of her!"

Kelsi gritted her teeth. She didn't want Taylor's exasperated support, either. She smiled tightly and said, "Oh, well, that's Sharpay. Listen, I'd better get going. I have tons of homework to do, and my mom wants me to start dinner tonight, and I'm working on a new song . . ." Her voice trailed off as she saw, from the expressions on her friends' faces, that they weren't buying any of these excuses. "Anyway," she finished rather lamely, "I'll see you guys tomorrow."

She left the gym as quickly as she could. Gabriella watched her leave and then said, "Guys, we've got to do a better job than this if we want our plan to work."

Taylor cast an accusing glance at Chad and added, "I thought you were going to help your good buddy, Jean-Luc. Why didn't you say something to get him out of Sharpay's clutches?"

Chad shrugged helplessly and said, "Sorry! Come on, we're up against Sharpay here! My mind went blank!"

"How unusual," Taylor muttered. Gabriella bit her lip to keep from laughing.

"Not to worry," Troy said. "I've got an idea."

CHAPTER SEVEN

Chad watched the clock as the minutes ticked down to the last bell on Tuesday afternoon. He and Troy were about to embark on a mission to save Jean-Luc from Sharpay. He was wholeheartedly committed to the cause, but he wasn't foolish enough to think it would be easy. Sharpay was clearly determined to stay close to Jean-Luc for the rest of his visit.

He glanced across the aisle and caught Troy's eye. Troy gave a slight nod, keeping his face

107

blank, just the way spies and con artists did in all those cool caper movies. Chad looked away hastily. Sharpay was sitting on the other side of Troy. He didn't want her to suspect that anything was up.

He went back to staring at the clock. Only three minutes left before the end of the school day.

His gaze slid sideways to watch Sharpay. She was staring dreamily into space and twirling a long piece of hair between her fingers. Chad didn't need to be a mind reader to know who she was thinking about.

The minute hand jumped. Two minutes to go.

Troy caught Chad's eye and made a little circle with his index finger, reminding his friend that he needed to move fast when the bell rang. Chad nodded and closed his notebook, getting ready for action.

One minute to go.

He tensed.

The bell rang.

The room erupted with noise as everybody slammed their books closed, pushed their chairs back, and started talking to their friends as they moved eagerly toward the door. Because he had been alert and ready to go, Chad had a head start—only a few seconds, but it was enough for him to scoot up the aisle and get to the door in front of Sharpay.

Right on cue, he dropped his textbook and notebook. Papers scattered everywhere. He blocked the door as he knelt to gather them up.

"What are you doing?" Sharpay demanded, trying without success to push past him. "Get out of the way! I have a very urgent appointment! It's incredibly important to my career. *Absolutely vital*, in fact."

"Sorry, sorry," Chad said. He managed to actually sound sorry, which he secretly thought was quite an impressive acting feat. In fact, it was as impressive as anything Sharpay had ever done on the stage.

He stood up, clutching his papers, and turned

just enough to let Troy slip past. Then he dropped everything again.

"Oh, no, I don't know what's wrong with me!" he cried dramatically as he stooped to pick up his things for a second time.

"At least move out of the way so the rest of us can leave!" Sharpay snapped.

"I'm doing my best," Chad said, whining a little even as he fumbled with the papers and dropped them for a third time. "No one can ask for more than that."

"I can!" Sharpay said, exasperated. She craned her neck to peer into the hallway. "I need to go meet—"

From his crouching position, Chad followed her gaze just in time to see Troy and Jean-Luc disappearing through the door at the end of the hall.

"Jean-Luc!" Sharpay finished her sentence, a note of disbelief in her voice. "But where is he *going*?"

Chad finally stood up and moved out of the

way. "I don't know," he said innocently. "Maybe he has a very urgent, incredibly important, absolutely vital appointment, too."

Troy and Jean-Luc burst through the front doors into the fresh air. Jean-Luc stopped and turned to Troy. "Thank you very much," he said. "I would not have been able to avoid Sharpay on my own."

"Not a problem," Troy said. He glanced back through the doors, then patted Jean-Luc on the shoulder. "But now you'd better go. Chad won't be able to stop Sharpay for long. She could be out here any minute. Kelsi's going to meet you at the theater downtown, the one that shows art films. Here are the directions."

Jean-Luc took the paper from Troy and grinned. "Thank you again, *mon ami*."

"You're welcome," Troy said, grinning back. "Have a good time!"

For the rest of the week, Troy, Chad, Gabriella, and Taylor worked together like a team of top-notch spies. Their mission: stop Sharpay.

Taylor sent Sharpay a text message that made her cell phone ring in homeroom, earning both of them detention, a sacrifice Taylor was willing to make for the greater good of getting Kelsi and Jean-Luc together.

Chad taught Jean-Luc several shortcuts through the school. That helped Jean-Luc avoid Sharpay and meet Kelsi for pizza one day after school.

Taylor and Gabriella suggested to Ms. Darbus that the Drama Club should make more use of the beautiful Parisian backdrop by performing a play about Impressionist painters in 1890s France. Sharpay was immediately cast as one of the leads and was kept busy with extra rehearsals for several afternoons.

When Sharpay once managed to leave rehearsal in time to catch the end of basketball practice, Chad quickly convinced Ryan to help their cause. Jean-Luc ducked into the locker room, changed from his basketball uniform into the Wiley the Wildcat costume, and escaped from the gym right under Sharpay's nose.

Troy even told Jean-Luc about the rooftop garden, his favorite spot in the school, and Gabriella told Kelsi. Then Gabriella generously offered to help Sharpay write a note to Jean-Luc in French, but she spent such a long time making it perfect that Jean-Luc was nowhere to be found when Sharpay went looking for him. Strangely enough, Kelsi was also noticeably absent.

By the end of the week, Sharpay was practicing a new song for the competition, rehearsing the lead role in a new play, and serving occasional detentions. The one thing she wasn't doing, much to the team's satisfaction, was spending any time with Jean-Luc.

CHAPTER EIGHT

On Friday afternoon, the auditorium was packed with eager spectators watching their classmates compete in the talent show.

"Thank you, Clarissa, for that moving monologue from your play, *Singing the Sophomore Blues*," Principal Matsui said. He was standing at the microphone onstage, acting as emcee for the talent show. "I'm sure we'll all look forward to seeing a full production soon. Now remember, we have a decibel monitor backstage to register how much applause each performer receives. The act that gets the loudest applause wins, which means that *you* are our judges. So let's give it up for Clarissa, everybody!"

A dutiful wave of applause rippled through the auditorium. Principal Matsui looked at the member of the tech crew who was backstage monitoring the applause decibels earned by each act. Then he turned back to the audience. "All right!" he said. "Clarissa just registered a 6.2, which puts her in third place!"

Troy leaned over to whisper to Gabriella, "Did you talk to Kelsi before she had to go backstage? Is she nervous?"

Gabriella smiled and shook her head. "No, not at all. I think she's had other things on her mind this week besides the competition!"

Taylor, who was sitting with Chad one row in front of Troy and Gabriella, overheard them. She turned her head to add, "You know, if I didn't know how shy Kelsi can be, I would have said she seemed a little smug today. She said something to me right before lunch about having a big surprise for everyone this afternoon."

The four of them exchanged puzzled glances.

"Really," Troy said. "That sounds kind of . . . *dramatic* for Kelsi, doesn't it?"

"Maybe she's going to take Sharpay on!" Chad suggested. "Maybe she's going to go full-blown diva on us! Maybe we're going to see a talent show smackdown!"

Gabriella giggled at Chad's joking, but Taylor said coolly, "Maybe we should be quiet for a few seconds. The next act is about to come on."

Onstage, Principal Matsui cleared his throat and grabbed the mic, causing an ear-piercing shriek to echo through the room. After a few seconds, he managed to stop the feedback long enough to say, "I think you'll all agree that we've already enjoyed a pretty wide range of talents this afternoon. You may think that it would be difficult to give a performance that would be unique. But you would be wrong! So now for something completely different, I offer you the gymnastic stylings of Wiley the Wildcat!"

"Is this what Kelsi was talking about?" Gabriella whispered as the lights went down.

"I don't think so," Troy whispered back. "Although it *is* surprising . . ."

The auditorium went completely dark. Then several spotlights bathed the stage in light. The pulsing beat of reggae music filled the air. And Wiley the Wildcat came springing from the wing of the stage, doing a series of backflips exactly on the beat!

The mascot ended up at center stage, his arms held high in the air. The audience began clapping and whistling in appreciation of his athletic opening, but Wiley didn't stop there. He began doing cartwheels, flips, and splits. He jumped in the air and executed a 360-degree spin; he dove toward the floor, landed on his hands, and catapulted himself into the air; he did a few pop-and-lock dance moves and then pulled a girl from the audience to dance with him.

By the end of the song, the crowd was on its feet, clapping along. As the last note rang out, Wiley took a quick bow, cartwheeled offstage, and was gone.

"That was fantastic!" Taylor said.

"I never knew the furry little dude could move like that," Chad agreed.

Before they could discuss it further, Principal Matsui was back at the mic. "Thank you, Ryan Evans, for that performance—and thank you, Andrew Everline, for the choreography! Let's get you both out here for another round of applause!"

Andrew limped onstage, followed by Ryan, who had taken off his Wildcat head but was still wearing the rest of his costume. They raised their hands triumphantly and grinned as the auditorium erupted into cheers. As they left the stage, Mr. Matsui continued, "I just got word that Ryan and Andrew's entry has received a 9.9 on the decibel monitor, which puts them in first place! Now I'd like to introduce another talented member of the Evans family, someone you all know very well, Miss Sharpay Evans!"

The curtain was pulled back to reveal Sharpay standing still, dressed in a sparkly silver and blue costume. The stage crew had done a masterful job of creating a Paris street scene on the backdrop, complete with twinkling lights. The slow, sad strains of a French ballad came from the speakers, and Sharpay began to sing.

After Ryan's energetic performance, the crowd was buzzing with excitement. Still, by the time Sharpay reached the second line of the song, she had managed to change the mood of the auditorium from that of a high-spirited pep rally to a small, quiet café somewhere in Paris. As she softly sang the last note, a hush fell over the auditorium for several seconds. Then a surge of clapping filled the room, and Sharpay took her bows with a self-satisfied smile.

As Gabriella clapped, she said to Troy, "You know, Sharpay may be a little self-involved at times, but you have to admit—"

"She has tons of talent," Troy said, nodding. "There's no doubt about that!"

Onstage, Principal Matsui mopped his forehead. "Sharpay Evans just earned—" he paused dramatically, "a 9.9! Yes, you heard me right, East High! We now have a tie for first place, and we still have one more performance to go!"

Taylor turned around again. "I hope Kelsi's not getting nervous backstage," she said. "It's tough to hear how well everyone else does when you're still waiting for your turn."

Everyone looked worried at this thought, but a piano was being rolled onstage and Kelsi was walking out from the wings, followed by . . . Jean-Luc! Carrying a cello!

Surprised whispers filled the air.

"This must be the surprise Kelsi was talking about!" Gabriella said, delighted.

Sure enough, Mr. Matsui introduced the pair by saying, "And to close our show, I'd like to introduce Miss Kelsi Nielsen and Monsieur Jean-Luc Laurent, performing an original duet that they composed themselves."

Kelsi sat at the piano bench and exchanged a shy glance with Jean-Luc. He smiled at her as he sat on his chair and placed his bow on the cello strings. There was a slight pause as they gazed at each other—then Kelsi began playing. After a few notes, Jean-Luc joined her on the cello. Together, they wove a spell, playing a song that was haunting and mysterious, with some sections that sounded joyous and others that sounded sad, yet all twining together into a complete and perfect whole.

By the end, it seemed that Kelsi and Jean-Luc had completely forgotten about the audience. They seemed to be playing only for each other. The sight and sound of a standing ovation brought them back to where they were: onstage in front of the whole school, being cheered on by their friends. They grinned at each other and took quick bows before running off into the wings.

Principal Matsui ducked backstage to double-check the decibel monitor readout for each performance.

"That was amazing," Troy said.

"Yeah, it was," Chad agreed. "And I don't even know anything about music!"

Gabriella and Taylor exchanged sly looks. Their matchmaking scheme had worked better than they could have hoped. Not only did Kelsi and Jean-Luc fall for each other, but they had just brought down the house with their performance!

Sure enough, when Mr. Matsui emerged from backstage to announce the winner of the competition, the results didn't surprise anyone. . . .

"Kelsi! Congratulations!" Gabriella ran up to her friend and threw her arms around her.

"Yeah, way to go, girl," Taylor said, right behind her. "First place is awesome!"

Kelsi was smiling more widely and blushing more deeply than ever. "Thanks," she said. "If it hadn't been for you guys—"

"We would not have had all that time to work on our music," Jean-Luc finished, with just a hint of mischief in his eyes. "Indeed, I, too, must say *merci beaucoup.*"

"Glad to help out, buddy," Troy said, slapping him on the back.

"Yeah, no thanks necessary," Chad said, punching him on the shoulder. "But listen, we need to work in some basketball practice pretty soon. I've still got some moves to teach you before you go back to France."

"Of course, I am most interested in learning more moves," Jean-Luc said. "And in watching you play this evening."

Taylor put her hand to her head, pretending to be shocked. "Oh, no, is that tonight?" she cried. "Did I actually forget something as important as a basketball game?"

"Don't worry, Chad wouldn't let it slip your mind for long," Troy said, grinning.

"Neither would I!" Ryan had bounded up to them just in time to hear the end of the conversation. "Wait till you see what Andrew and I have planned for tonight's performance!"

He was beaming, as was Andrew, who followed slowly in his wake. "It will make today's show look like amateur hour," Andrew promised.

"The talent show will be hard to match," Gabriella said. "You guys totally deserved first prize!"

"I'm glad there was a tie," Ryan said to Kelsi and Jean-Luc. "It's amazing that we got exactly the same decibel count! Especially since—"

"My applause registered the same number as yours," Sharpay interrupted. She was standing a few feet away, looking uncharacteristically unsure of herself. "Of course, it's ridiculous to compare the work of a *chanteuse* such as myself to an instrumental duet or a gymnastic demonstration—"

Ryan raised one eyebrow and waited.

"Although I must say that I've never seen a crowd respond to a performance the way they did to what you two did," she went on, with a nod to Ryan and Andrew. "One might even say that it reached the level of . . . art."

They grinned at each other. To anyone else, Sharpay's words might have sounded grudging, but they knew an apology when they heard one.

"And I do have another first place award to add to my collection at home," Sharpay added, placing the medal around her neck. It glinted gold in the light, matching the medals that hung around the necks of Kelsi, Jean-Luc, Ryan, and Andrew. "Pretty soon I'm going to have to ask Daddy to enlarge the trophy room!"

Everyone rolled their eyes at that, but they were all smiling.

"What do you say we all go out after the game to celebrate?" Gabriella suggested.

"I say yes!" Jean-Luc said. "Or as we say in France—"

"*Mais oui!*" everyone chorused together, laughing.

Look for an exciting new Super Special in the
High School Musical: Stories From East High series!

SHINING MOMENTS

By Sarah Nathan
Based on the Disney Channel Original Movie
"High School Musical," Written by Peter Barsocchini
Based on "High School Musical 2," Written by Peter Barsocchini
Based on Characters Created by Peter Barsocchini

The East High seniors are superbusy during the last few weeks of school leading up to graduation. They are volunteering at the local community center for their senior project and are gearing up for a huge graduation party at the Lava Springs Country Club! Sharpay couldn't be more excited—she gets to direct a musical for her volunteer assignment! But when her production needs a major overhaul, and Taylor and Chad stop speaking, the rest of the Wildcats realize they need to work together more than ever!